Mother Knows Best

Netta Newbound

Junction Publishing
New Zealand

Copyright © 2014 by Netta Newbound.

All rights reserved. No part of this publication may be reproduced, distributed or transmitted in any form or by any means, including photocopying, recording, or other electronic or mechanical methods, without the prior written permission of the publisher, except in the case of brief quotations embodied in critical reviews and certain other noncommercial uses permitted by copyright law. For permission requests, write to the publisher, addressed "Attention: Permissions Coordinator," at the email address below.

Netta Newbound/ Junction Publishing
Waihi 3610
New Zealand
nettanewbound@hotmail.com
www.nettanewbound.com

Publisher's Note: This is a work of fiction. Names, characters, places, and incidents are a product of the author's imagination. Locales and public names are sometimes used for atmospheric purposes. Any resemblance to actual people, living or dead, or to businesses, companies, events, institutions, or locales is completely coincidental.

Book Layout & Design ©2013 - BookDesignTemplates.com

Ordering Information:
Quantity sales. Special discounts are available on quantity purchases by corporations, associations, and others. For details, contact the "Special Sales Department" at the email address above.

Mother Knows Best/ Netta Newbound. -- 1st ed.
ISBN 978-1503202696

To my wonderful mother, Lynda, whose intuition and perception never fail to astound me.

My mother had a great deal of trouble with me, but I think she enjoyed it ...
Mark Twain

Chapter 1

The cold dank air hit her nostrils like a sledgehammer. Ruby recoiled. Froze. Held her breath. After a few minutes, she tried to turn her head. Immense pain shot through her temples, settling to a dull throb at the base of her skull. She fought to keep her eyes open—needing to remember where the hell she was. She couldn't. She gave in to the heavy, drifting sensation.

Ruby opened her eyes not sure how much time had passed. She reached up to touch the tender spot on the back of her head. A cry escaped her as a thick stickiness came away on her fingertips. The metallic scent of blood now mingled with the earthy, wet stench surrounding her.

She shivered as blood gushed through her veins in unison with the thudding inside her head.

She could see nothing. Not a thing.

Were her eyes even open?

She knew they were when she felt them close.

The only sound was the continuous drip-drip-drip that came from all around her.

She managed to roll onto her back. Icy rock touched her on either side. She reached up and yelped as the tips of her fingers hit more hard rock not six inches above her face.

She was in a tunnel—a cold, dark tunnel.

Thirty hours earlier ...

Baxter, the scruffy eight-month-old Border terrier, spun on the spot when Ruby arrived home. It didn't matter if she'd been gone for five minutes or five hours, the welcome was always the same.

"Hello, my favourite four legged friend. I missed you too." Ruby dropped to her haunches to pet him.

Baxter launched himself into her arms, sending Ruby crashing backwards onto the kitchen tiles.

"You dozy sausage." She tried to bat the dog away.

Taking advantage of his owner's accessible position on the floor, Baxter pounced and licked her face.

Ruby squealed as dog tongue slipped between her lips and lapped at her mouth and teeth. She gagged in between hysterical laughter.

Ruby got to her feet and poured some kibble into Baxter's dish. While he was occupied, she ran upstairs to fill the bath. After rummaging through her wardrobe, in search of an outfit for her date, she settled on a floral cotton dress. She held the dress in front of her and checked in the mirror. It was perfect for the balmy summer evening. She smiled at her reflection. The cornflower blue petals set off her eyes.

After getting undressed, she grabbed her phone from the bedside cabinet and headed to the bathroom. Once submerged in the deep bubbly water—one arm held aloft—she pressed redial.

Her sister, Scarlett, picked up on the second ring. "Hi Rubes, I wondered if you would call before your big date—are you all set?"

"No, but he's not picking me up until eight. I'm nervous though. This is my first date since David, what if I can't think of anything to say?"

Scarlett's throaty giggle sounded at the other end of the phone.

"What's so funny?"

"You! Lost for words—there's more danger of you chewing his ears off."

"Cheeky bitch!" Ruby laughed too.

"Besides, I thought you had loads in common with what's-his-name?"

"Cody. Well, he's into walking, like me. He has one pain in the neck younger sister, also like me."

"Hey!"

Ruby laughed. "Other than that, he could be a mass murderer for all I know."

"Don't let Mum hear you say that, whatever you do. She wouldn't let me out the door last night without interrogating Mathew first. She's still going on about the Felicity girl who vanished months ago. I wouldn't be surprised if she's gone off to Spain or somewhere. I bet she's shacked up with her boyfriend, having a wonderful time. No school—no nagging."

"I don't think so, sis. Don't you watch the news?" In her mind's eye, Ruby saw the image of a delicate, blond haired, sixteen-year-old girl who had been all over the TV and newspapers for the past three months. In the photograph, Felicity wore the same multi-coloured woollen jersey she had gone missing in.

"Of course I do. Mum makes me—she's obsessed."

"She worries, that's all. She's right to."

"Say's you. You're off out tonight with a stranger—I don't see you getting the third degree."

"I've left home. It's a bit different."

"Not really. Like you said, he could be a mass murderer. I might just tell Mum for the hell of it—get the heat off me for a change."

"Don't you dare, Scarlett, I was kidding. He's a normal fella I met at the gym—I've seen him loads of times."

"Text me once you're home so I know you're safe, then."

"Will do, sis. Speak later."

***

Legs and underarms shaved, Ruby pulled the bath plug out just as the phone rang. She checked the caller ID—her mother. "Bloody Scarlett," Ruby said.

She considered not answering, but knew her mother would continue ringing all night until she got to speak to her eldest daughter. No—the easiest thing would be to get it over and done with.

"Hang on a sec, Mum," Ruby said as she stepped from the bath. She placed the phone on the sink, reached for a towel and dried herself, wrapping her hair in a towel. She picked up the phone once more. "I'm back."

"Scarlett tells me you're going out on a date." In an irate voice, her mother confirmed her treacherous sister was the reason for the call.

Ruby rolled her eyes and gave a loud sigh.

"Don't be like that, dear. I worry is all."

"There's no need to worry, Mum. He's a nice young man I met at the gym."

"Does he work?"

"Yes ..."

"Well?"

"He's self-employed—something to do with computers."

"Where does he live?"

"I'm not sure. Around here somewhere. It didn't cross my mind to ask for his address to give to my mother." Ruby laughed.

"How about a name? Anything will do."

"I told Scarlett his name and I said I'd text her once I get home. I'm twenty-two years old—I'm not a baby anymore."

"I never said you were—anyway, what difference does your age make? I'll still worry about you when you're sixty. My mother still worries about me."

"I know she does, Mum. Listen, I've got to go. I'll be fine—I promise. I'll see you tomorrow, it's market day, remember?" Her mother's protests rang out until Ruby ended the call.

Ruby felt bad for cutting her mother off, but this had been the same since Ruby was a young girl.

Her mother was convinced that either she or Scarlett would end up dead in a ditch. The thought of this had freaked them out for a long time. After all, they'd had it drummed into their head's that Mother knows best, so if she believed they would come to a sticky end, it must be true.

So Ruby resisted putting herself into a position where she could become a victim, never meeting new people or staying away from home. She even dated the boy next door, David, who seemed to have her mother's approval. But eventually, her mother's paranoia became too much even for him.

The final straw had been when her mother stopped them from going to his cousin's wedding. He said he loved her but couldn't live with her mother's continual interference. And so, in the nicest possible way, he dumped her.

Heartbroken, Ruby accused her mother of breaking them up and soon after, she left home. The best thing she ever did.

Wait until she got her hands on that trouble causing sister of hers. She would throttle her.

She rushed through to the bedroom. After one last rub down with the towel, she sprayed copious amounts of deodorant under her arms before slipping into the dress.

Leaving her shoulder length brown hair to air dry, Ruby ran a mascara wand over her lashes and a dab of gloss to her red lips—the reason for her name. Her dad said her ruby red lips were the first things he noticed when she was less than a minute old and the name was chosen.

Scarlett's name came about to fit in with the trend—no real reason behind it. It had been a standing joke within the family that if they'd gone on to have a boy they'd have named him something ridiculous like Burnt-Orange or Lime-Green—or even plain old Red.

Baxter whimpered when he realised Ruby was going out again. She still had over half an hour so she made herself a cup of coffee and sat on the sofa with the little dog.

"Hey, sweetie, it's okay—I won't be late." She rubbed his side and giggled when his back leg scratched mid-air, his eyes rolling in ecstasy. She hated leaving him alone when she'd already been gone all day. She needed a social life, otherwise her life would be nothing but work-work-work. And although she loved her job, she needed a balance, or what was the point?

Her job at the local council wasn't anything exciting. As receptionist, she was the first target for any abuse or negativity, either by phone or in person. As happens in any government department worldwide. Nevertheless, she tried to make a difference—always going the extra mile for members of the public whenever she could.

Ruby swilled her empty coffee cup under the tap. She no longer fancied a night out, would much prefer an evening snuggled in front of the TV with Baxter. But her date was due in a few minutes so she'd best get ready sharpish.

After one last swish of the dress in front of the mirror, she slipped her feet into high-heeled, cream coloured sandals, folded a cotton cardigan over her arm and waited by the window.

When a small white car pulled up outside, Ruby's stomach clenched. She gave Baxter a final scratch under the chin before she headed from the small terraced house and tottered across the pavement to the car.

Cody jumped out, ran around the car and opened the passenger door for her.

Ruby noticed how different he looked in his smart dress trousers and short-sleeved lemon cotton shirt. She'd only ever seen him in his gym gear before.

As she climbed into the passenger seat, Ruby's bag vibrated and played a tune alerting her of a text message. She retrieved her mobile from her small bag and read it—Mum.

Scarlett doesn't have the boy's details. Send them through to me please—it's important. Sorry to be a pest, but Mother knows best.

Ruby rolled her eyes at her mother's attempt at humour.

Chapter 2

Cody's cock twitched when Ruby emerged from her front door. She looked gorgeous in the floaty summer dress she wore. He'd chosen well this time. His father thought she might be too old, but he'd soon eat his words when he set eyes on her. Cody was certain.

Ever the gentleman, Cody raced around the car and held the door open while his date slid into the passenger seat. She was looking at her phone when he got in beside her.

"Anything important?" he asked, nodding at her phone as she put it back into her bag.

"What? Oh no—just my mum—she's such a stress-head. She refuses to accept I'm an adult." She laughed.

As Cody drove away, he noticed a woman peeking from the window opposite.

"You're lucky she cares. I barely remember my mum—she died when I was a kid."

"Oh, I'm sorry, I didn't mean ..."

"You didn't, don't worry." He smiled.

"I lost my dad, so I know the pain of losing a parent. You do still have your dad, don't you?" She braced herself, her hand in the centre of her chest, praying she hadn't made a double booboo.

"Yes." He laughed. "He's still with us, in fact, he brought up my brother Kyle and me single-handed."

"Your brother? I thought you only had a sister?" Ruby's brow furrowed as she glanced at him.

Cody's stomach clenched. Annoyed with himself for being so stupid—he normally stuck as close to the truth as possible.

"No—a younger brother, Kyle, but we call him Kylie. You see he intends to have a sex change operation as soon as he's old enough."

"Really? Ruby said with a wide-eyed stare.

"Yup. So I often say he's my sister, to avoid confusion when the time comes."

"What does your dad think?"

Cody shrugged. "He's fine. To be honest, it's always been obvious to us since he was little." He marvelled at how easy the lies flew off his tongue.

"Poor thing, that sounds horrendous, and without a mother to help him through it, too."

"He's okay—made of tough stuff just like anybody who's a bit different in this day and age needs to be."

"I guess." Ruby turned to gaze through the side window.

After a few minutes of silence, they both began talking at the same time.

"I'm sorry, you go," Ruby said.

"It's okay—you first."

"I was going to ask where we're going?"

"There's a quaint little pub towards the coast, if you don't mind the drive, that is? It shouldn't take too long."

"No—not at all. It makes a change to get out of town—I rarely do," she said, a faraway look in her eye.

Delicious bubbles of excitement filled his stomach. She was perfect.

They made small talk as they drove. Her phone buzzed several more times and he realised this could cause him a problem. He needed to think this through.

"How long have you lived in Penderton?" he asked.

"All my life. My dad's family owned the house my mum still lives in. She did consider selling up after dad died but couldn't go through with it in the end."

"How did he die?"

She shrugged. "An accident. It would be funny if not so tragic."

"Why, what happened?"

"He choked on a chicken bone." She half smiled. "No-one was home at the time and he'd raided the fridge. Mum and I found him on the kitchen floor when I was nine years old. He'd been dead for hours."

"That's shocking." Cody glanced at her, his eyebrows drawn together.

They pulled into a pub car park.

"It was—anyway, let's change the subject." She sat forward in her seat.

Her phone buzzed again.

"Somebody's keen."

"My mum again. I'll text her back once we get inside otherwise she'll be at it all night."

The place was pumping as Cody had predicted it would be—less chance of anybody noticing them this way. He spotted a middle-aged couple preparing to leave and so he hovered by their table and quickly guided Ruby to the booth as they left. He piled their empty plates and glasses and shoved them into the far corner.

A steady hum of chatter surrounded them—Cody couldn't even tell if any music played in the background. He gestured to Ruby to ask if she wanted a drink.

She nodded and mouthed cider.

From his position at the bar, he watched as she sent a text message. "Bugger," he muttered under his breath.

Once he had the drinks, he made his way back to the table. A large blond haired man, who could have just stepped off a rugby pitch, blocked his way and made a production of not allowing him to pass. Cody managed to dart around him, but clocked the fierce expression in the big man's eyes.

He slid behind the table next to Ruby. "Is Mum happy again?" he asked.

"She'll never be happy, but now she knows where I am, we should get a bit of peace," she laughed.

Cody tipped his head back in acknowledgement, still smiling—at least on the outside. His dad would have a fit when he found out—but he couldn't stop her contacting her mother without looking like a complete psycho. He would deal with it later.

Chapter 3

Ruby could have strangled her mother. Her phone buzzed continually the whole journey. Once she got to the pub, she snatched it from her bag and read five new messages.

- Did you get my last text?
- Ruby Fitzroy, answer me immediately. I'm worried.
- Please text Mum – she's driving me mad – Soz sis x
- WHERE ARE YOU?
- Why are you punishing me like this? If you don't reply, I'll call.

Ruby hit reply.

- Mother please get the hint – Stop nagging! I'm having a great time with Cody. We are in a pub close to the coast. NO MORE MESSAGES.

Letting out an angry sigh, she stuffed the phone back into her bag. She glanced up and noticed an altercation with Cody and a large wall of a guy. Moments later, skirmish avoided, Cody slid in beside her.

This was her first date since David, and although she'd spent the past twelve months waiting for him to call, she accepted he never would and had decided to get on with her life.

There was something about Cody she liked a lot. Not just his looks, although his shaggy blond hair and deep blue eyes were to die for. But when he told her about his poor brother—or indeed, sister situation, her heart missed a beat. Nothing was more appealing to her than a sensitive man.

He even seemed to understand about her mum. It was still early days, but she had a good feeling about him.

"I hope you're hungry," Cody said.

A large group of people left and although the place was still noisy, she could now hear Cody's voice.

"Starving."

"Good, because I ordered us both burger and chips—there wasn't much of a selection. I hope you don't mind."

"Not at all. Sounds lovely," she said, sipping her cider.

The rest of the evening ran smoothly. They devoured their food and drinks. Because of the noise, they huddled together in order to hear each other. But Ruby wasn't complaining.

Cody poured his heart out about his mother—she had vanished without a trace when Cody was four years old, his brother only two. How, after a massive search the police had found nothing at all. She was declared dead when he was eleven years old. He told her about his obsession with football and how his dream of playing for Swansea ended at the UK trials when he suffered a hamstring injury.

Ruby had never felt such a connection with another person—apart from David of course, but she'd known him all her life. She didn't want the evening to end and her heart sank when Cody picked his car keys up from the table.

"We'd best get going," he said.

She sighed, and followed him to the exit.

As they stepped onto the porch, the blond man from earlier appeared—blocking their way.

Ruby squealed and grasped Cody's upper arm with both hands.

"Well, look who it is," the larger man said.

"Listen man, I don't want any trouble—we were just having a quiet drink."

"Who said I want trouble? I'm after an apology—you threw your drink down my jacket earlier."

"No I didn't."

"Are you calling me a liar?" The man's voice boomed.

"Of course not, but I didn't spill my drink."

"So what do you call this then? Scotch mist?" He pointed to the front of his jacket.

Ruby couldn't see anything.

"Listen, mate. If I accidentally spilt my drink—I'm sorry. I didn't mean to. Now can you let us pass?"

"So, you're admitting you did it?" The man's lip curled as he spoke.

Ruby could hear her heartbeat in her ears. She'd never experienced anything like this in her life.

"No—I'm saying *if* I did, I'm sorry," Cody said.

"Why apologise then, if you're innocent?" The man stepped forward, prodding a large sausage-like finger in Cody's chest.

"What do you want me to say? I didn't mean to spill my drink down you, but if I did, I'm sorry." Cody put an arm around Ruby's shoulders and tried to manoeuvre them both around the huge brute.

"Hey! Where do you think you're going? The man's arm shot out blocking their way once more.

Before she knew what had happened, Ruby flew backwards hitting the door with a bang. When she managed to right herself, Cody was up against the wall, his nose bleeding and the guy standing over him.

Several men seemed to appear from nowhere and managed to bundle the blond guy away.

Ruby ran to Cody's side. "Oh my God—are you alright?"

Cody held a hand below his nose catching most of the blood, although several large splashes had made it down the front of his shirt.

"I'm okay," he said. In fact, the exact words were I'bokay, but Ruby knew what he meant.

"Let's get you back inside—clean you up." She escorted him to the men's toilet and he went inside alone. He emerged a few minutes later looking more composed.

"You need to get that shirt in to soak—it'll be ruined if not," Ruby said.

"Do you mind if we pop to my dad's on the way home? He lives close by."

"Course not. Are you sure you can drive though? I don't have a licence."

"I'll be fine, come on."

Back outside, Ruby's nerves were so tightly wound she almost ran to the car expecting the big man to appear around every parked car they passed. But the parking area was once again deserted.

Safely in the car, Cody turned into the street heading in the opposite direction they came from. He held a large wad of toilet tissue to his face.

"Are you okay?" Ruby asked.

"Uh-huh."

"Do you want me to call your dad? What if he's not at home?"

"I have a key, but he'll be home. He never goes out."

Cody turned the car away from the coast into a winding gravel road. The trees alongside were dense and the huge branches created a leafy arch across the road.

The eeriness gave Ruby the shivers. "Is it much further?" Her voice sounded whiny to her own ears.

"Uh-huh." He shook his head.

Her heart raced in her chest and prickles forming at the base of her neck developed into goose bumps which covered her entire body.

Cody must have sensed her unease as he glanced at her. He dropped the tissue into his lap and reached for her hand. "It's okay, don't worry." He smiled.

Ruby pointed at the large drop of blood growing rapidly at the end of his nose.

He grabbed the tissue and caught the blood before it fell.

"We should call the police. That brute needs locking up," she said.

"There's no point—the police won't do anything."

"He can't be allowed to go around smashing innocent people's faces in just for the sake of it."

"I'll get him back—don't you worry."

Ruby wasn't sure if he was acting all macho in front of her. She had just witnessed him getting his arse kicked after all. But the way he said it, combined with the icy cold glint in his eyes, Ruby wasn't so sure.

"Where is this place?" The car had slowed as it began climbing the steep hill. "It's freaky."

Cody laughed. "It must seem that way, seeing it in the dark for the first time, but it's not—it's quite beautiful. All this land used to belong to a mining company. Dad bought it off them before we were born. I've lived here all my life."

"Your dad owns all this?"

"Yup. I only moved into town recently, but I come back here whenever I get the chance."

As they reached the top of the hill, Cody took a sharp turn to the left and moments later a two-story stone house came into view.

The house was lit up like a Chinese lantern, every room illuminated from within and the porch light also came on as they approached.

Ruby breathed a sigh of relief. "Your dad's electricity bill must be shocking." She laughed.

"I know, it is. I'm always going around after them both turning off the lights." He shook his head.

"Shall I wait here?"

"No, don't be daft. Come on in."

"But it's late—won't your dad mind?"

"No. He's not like that—he'll be pleased to meet you."

"Well, if you're sure."

"Certain," he said and walked around to her side to open the door.

A large grey cat skulked in the shadows, startling Ruby as its eyes flashed.

"Don't mind Wesley, he's harmless." Cody took a step towards the cat, making a hissing sound and the cat vanished into the bushes.

Feeling self-conscious, Ruby followed Cody into the porch.

He unlocked the door. "It's only me," he called as he stepped into the spacious hallway.

Considering three men lived there, Ruby was surprised how neat and tidy everywhere was.

A large plastic bin to the side of the front door was filled with boots and shoes. The wall opposite the staircase held a painting of a man's head and upper body. Although the painting was brightly coloured, the green eyes held a darkness reminding Ruby of Dracula.

"Who's the artist?" Ruby asked.

"My brother."

"Wow! He's very good."

Cody stared at the painting as though seeing it for the first time. "Yes, I suppose he is."

Odd, thought Ruby.

The sound of a TV came from a room to the right.

Cody walked straight ahead into a large farmhouse style kitchen. The thick oak cupboard doors and large square porcelain sink looked like something from Home and Garden magazine.

Once again, Ruby was surprised by the neatness. She'd expected a house full of men to be in need of a good clean and a woman's touch—but not this house. In fact, it was tidier than her mum's house had been when three women lived there.

Chapter 4

Cody made Ruby a cup of tea before leaving her in the kitchen.

Instead of heading upstairs to change his shirt, first he went back out the front door and into the garage to the side of the house.

As he entered, his dad jumped off the makeshift bed.

"What the fuck happened to your face? Don't tell me—she got away."

"Calm down, Dad. She's in the kitchen having a cup of tea. I thought you might like to meet her—but leave the foul language out here, please."

"Why didn't you stick to the plan? And you still didn't tell me what happened."

"Some dick'ead decided to rearrange my face at the pub. But he did me a favour to be honest. Ruby didn't mind us coming up here afterwards, so she's none the wiser."

"Good."

"There is one problem, though," Cody said.

"What?" he screwed his eyes up and rubbed his temples.

"She told her mum where she was and who she was with."

"Fucking hell, lad. How're we gonna deal with that?"

"Don't worry, I have a plan. Trust me."

"Come on then. Let's get this over and done with."

They found Ruby sitting at the kitchen table sipping her tea.

"Ruby, this is my dad, Steve, Dad meet Ruby." Cody watched the older man's eyes light up.

"I'll leave you guys chatting while I grab a clean shirt," Cody said.

Ruby nodded, smiling.

Thudding music sounded out from another part of the house and in response to Ruby's confused expression his dad said, "My son, Kyle. Sorry, he has awful taste in music."

"Oh, Kylie?" Ruby asked.

Cody froze half in, half out of the door.

"Yeah, Cody told me about it," she said.

"Oh did he? Yes, Kylie," his dad said.

With a sigh, Cody ran up to his bedroom to change, certain the drugs he'd slipped into her tea should start working soon.

Half-way down the stairs, he heard a clatter. Heart racing, he jumped the remaining steps and ran into the kitchen.

Dad sat on the floor piling several baking trays and cake tins that had been strewn across the floor.

"What the ...?" Cody said.

"That bloody brother of yours, that's what. He's getting worse. This is the second time today I've had the entire contents of a cupboard throw themselves at me."

Cody turned to Ruby and smiled. "Kyle enjoys playing pranks on Dad. But Dad makes it so easy, wouldn't you say?"

Ruby smiled as she touched her temple. "I don't feel well—can you take me home, Cody, please?"

Cody jumped forward and caught Ruby as she slid from the chair.

Chapter 5

Cody's dad was delightful. Even though he had a good thirty years on his eldest son, they were the image of each other. The same mop of shaggy blond hair—although Steve's was tinged with grey—and identical deep blue eyes—albeit framed with several clusters of lines. She could have been looking at the same face in a time warp.

He pulled a chair out and sat opposite Ruby. Cody left the room.

"I presume you live in Penderton, Ruby?"

She nodded. "All my life. My mother owns one of the original cottages on Clark Street, off the old road."

"Ah, yes. I think old Bill used to live in one of them."

"Mr Grundy?"

"Yeah, old Bill Grundy. Do you know him?"

"I did—he died last year. I used to run errands for him as a kid."

"What a small world. I worked with him at the steelworks. He was my supervisor and mentor. I owe a lot of my skills to him."

"He never told me what he did for a living. He had been retired for as far back as I can remember. A lovely man though—always told lots of stories."

"He did that—he had a tough life—his wife died of lung cancer when his two kiddies were no more than knee high," he said.

"Really? I never heard about that."

"I have something here—look at this." Steve jumped off his chair and opened a cupboard door above the sink. All of a sudden, several trays and tins toppled out and fell to the floor, each one hitting him on the way down.

Ruby wasn't sure if it was surprise from the noise or delayed shock from the evening's events, but she came over all woozy.

Cody burst through the door as if ready for a fight—then stopped—relief flooding his face. He said something to Ruby then laughed, but she couldn't focus. What the hell was wrong with her?

She tried to get to her feet just as the kitchen floor fell away.

***

Her head thudded. She tried to open her eyes, but couldn't. She couldn't move at all.

She heard voices, but not the words. Her limbs had a heaviness she'd never experienced before—her eyelids too.

She eventually managed to open her eyes, but the stark white light-bulb above her head blinded her.

After a few moments her eyes adjusted to the light. Still thick-headed and confused, she tried to make sense of the cold whitewashed breezeblocks and the boarded up window. She still couldn't move, but this time, she realised why. Her hands and feet had been tied.

Sheer terror flooded her system and her screams filled the silence.

Chapter 6

"She's awake. Have you decided what we're gonna do?" Cody's dad said.

"Yes. We need to go back into town in two vehicles." Cody held up Ruby's keys and phone. "I'll sort it."

"I can't go out—there's Kyle to think about and not to mention ..."

"It's just a car-ride, Dad. You won't have to do anything else, I promise, and you'll be back before you know it."

"But what will you do? Once she's reported missing your name will be given to the police."

"I'll go to Jed's bar and make sure I'm seen by everyone. Then I'll go back to my flat—there's always a load of people there on Friday night, so at least I'll have an alibi."

"Don't come back here until it's sorted—the last thing we need is for the police to follow you."

"What do you think I am? An idiot? Course I won't lead anyone back here, but you've got to promise you won't touch her 'til I get back. Swear to me, Dad—not one finger, you hear me?"

"Loud and clear."

"And do you swear? She's mine first—I found her—them's the rules."

"Right! Stop fucking moaning."

Cody gripped the back of his dad's t-shirt and yanked him back, pushing his arm into the older man's throat. "I'm serious," he snarled.

His dad gulped and pushed at Cody's arm. "Alright, son—knock it off."

Cody released him. "Anyway, you still didn't tell me what you think of her?"

His dad nodded, brushing himself down. "Aye—you done good, son."

"She's perfect," Cody said, rubbing at his crotch. He had a good mind to go in there now and give her what for—but he couldn't—the first time had to be slow, so he could savour every second. No, he'd waited this long, another couple of days wouldn't make any difference. "Get Kyle to keep an eye on her while we're gone—I'll check she's properly tied—we don't want her to escape like the last one."

His father went inside the house and Cody into the garage.

Ruby twisted her whole body as he entered—her eyes reminiscent of a wild animal caught in a trap.

"Cody, help me. What's happening?"

"Ah, calm yourself, Ruby. Everything's going to be all right, but you must trust me—you do trust me, don't you, babe?"

Ruby nodded, although her stricken, terrified eyes told a different story.

"What's going on? Why am I tied up? Please Cody, let me go."

"No-can-do, sorry, babe. I've got to go away for a little while."

"No!" she shrieked.

"Shhhh." Cody sat on the edge of the bed and stroked her silky, brown hair. "I need you to calm down for me. Dad and Kyle will be here to look after you. When I get back, I promise things will be hunky-dory."

Ruby's whimpers were beginning to irritate the hell out of him, but he needed to keep his cool. He didn't want to spoil that pretty little face before he got some use out of her. He bent and kissed her forehead.

"Now, don't forget. Best behaviour until I get back."

Ruby stiffened and yanked her arms and legs as she cried. Her pleading eyes never left his face and her screams followed him out the door.

Cody found his dad and Kyle in the kitchen. "Have you told him?" he asked his dad.

"Yes-he-told-me," Kyle said, every word an effort as usual.

"Don't go in there, unless there's an emergency. Dad will be back soon. I need you to be in charge—look after her 'til I get back and I'll buy you a new fire truck."

"Bingo," Kyle said, holding both thumbs up.

"Good boy." He ruffled Kyle's hair before leaving.

Although only two years younger, Kyle had the mental age of a six-year-old. They sometimes left him alone for a short time, but not often. He needed a lot of looking after, one of the reasons their dad gave up work to care for him full-time after their mum vanished.

Kyle had seemed normal for the first year of his life, but when he still couldn't roll over or sit up unaided by his first birthday, the first warning bells sounded. Not that Cody could remember it, but he'd heard the story over and over.

Tests were done, but they had no explanation. They eventually diagnosed Kyle with an intellectual disability, or mentally retarded as they called it back then.

Kyle took his first step at two and a half years old, developing slowly. When he was eighteen, they were told his mental age wouldn't develop any further and it hadn't. But they wouldn't change him for the world.

Kyle had been a source of delight for Cody and their dad—always happy and playing pranks, although Kyle's obsession with fire trucks drove him to distraction.

Cody glanced in his rear-view mirror as he pulled over outside a row of shops at the end of Ruby's street, and climbed over to the passenger seat.

His dad parked his own car and then jumped in behind the wheel of Cody's.

"Right, where to?"

"It's down here on the left. I need you to wait until I get inside and switch on the light—then give several belts on the horn as you drive away."

"Got it," his dad said, before driving off.

Moments later, they pulled up outside Ruby's house. Cody turned off the interior lights, not wanting anybody to see him when he opened the door.

"Right, remember, park my car back up and leave the keys in the usual place."

His dad nodded. "Gotcha."

"I'm trusting you, Dad. Leave Ruby alone until I get back."

"I already said so, didn't I?"

"Right then—wait 'til I'm inside and the light goes on."

"Get on with it," his dad hissed.

Cody took Ruby's keys from his jacket pocket and picked her shoes up from the foot-well. Then, with a final bracing breath, he got out of the car.

Thanks to the late hour, the street was deserted. Cody opened the door and rushed inside slamming it behind him. Fumbling for a light switch, he was alarmed by something around his ankles. He tripped and fell to the carpet, landing on what he presumed was a cat until it yelped and began to snarl. A high-pitched *rrrrrrrr* turned into continual yapping. He needed to deal with it, but first he had to find a light.

Back on his feet, Cody located a light switch.

The little brown dog bared his teeth at Cody, just as a series of car horns sounded from outside.

Cody raced to the front window, peeking out. Sure enough—the curtain across the street twitched.

Pleased things were going according to plan, he turned back from the window.

"Now all I need to do is shut this fucking dog up.

Chapter 7

Still drowsy from whatever drugs they'd given her, Ruby felt like she was in a dream. Maybe it was a dream—or a sick joke and her mum would jump out any minute now after teaching her the greatest lesson of her life—always listen to your mother.

But it wasn't a dream *or* a joke. This was actually happening—every terrifying second of it.

The crunch of car tyres on gravel sounded soon after Cody left and she heard nothing but silence since.

Screaming had achieved nothing but to wear her out within minutes, causing her to drift off again.

She awoke to a scraping sound outside the door.

"Hello? Can anybody hear me? Help—please help," she called.

Nothing but silence.

Her eyes filled with tears and she shivered, her teeth chattering. Although the weather outside had been warm and muggy, the tiny room felt cold and damp.

Thick black plastic ties dug into her wrists and ankles causing her to wince every time she moved. The ties were threaded through chains anchored somewhere underneath the bed. She knew it would be pointless trying to unfasten them. The only way they were certain to move would be to tighten even more, cutting the blood supply off.

This situation was exactly what her mum had professed would happen—why the hell didn't she listen to her?

A tightness in her chest made it difficult to breathe and a pathetic whimper came from her throat. How would she escape this? Cody was clearly deranged, but Steve might help her.

"Steve?" she called. "Steve. Please help."

Nothing.

"Kyle—Kylie. Please."

Ruby's heartbeat thudded in her ears as the doorknob turned slowly. The anticipation was enough to kill her there and then. Who was it? She couldn't breathe—her eyes were trained on the opening door.

After what seemed like forever, a man appeared. His shaggy mop of blonde hair and sapphire blue eyes told her he was related to Cody and Steve.

"Kyle?"

"I'm-not-allowed-in," he said from the door. His voice sounded slow and slurred, every word ran into the next. He was nothing like Cody had described.

"It's okay, Kyle. I give you permission to come in—I need your help."

"Only-an-mergency."

"Yes, Kyle. This is an emergency."

"This-is-an-mergency?" Kyle tilted his head to one side, one eye half closed in confusion.

"Yes, I promise. This is an emergency."

"Okidoke-then." Kyle stepped into the room. "Do-you-like-my-fire-truck?" He shoved a bright red fire engine towards her.

"That's beautiful, Kyle." She didn't have time for this, but this odd man-child was her only hope of escape.

Kyle nodded as he studied the truck—a simple, sweet smile on his face.

"Kyle?"

Kyle pressed a button on the truck and a siren sounded.

"Kyle, can you help me?"

"Can't." Kyle shook his head and stepped backwards, a frightened expression clouded his face.

Ruby panicked. She knew she needed to get this overgrown child on side and fast.

"You know, my uncle is a fireman," she said, making her voice sound as bright as possible.

Kyle gasped. "A-real-fireman?"

"A real one. He's the driver," she said, smiling.

"Did-you-touched-it?"

"The fire engine? Yes, I touched it. I even had a ride in it."

Kyle's eyes bulged as Ruby watched the cogs turning in his brain.

"I bet I could get him to take you for a ride too. That is if you want to?"

"I-go-for-a-ride?" His excitement was almost palpable.

"Uh-huh. If you could help me get out of here."

Kyle's expression clouded once more. "Can't." He shook his head.

"Please, Kyle." Ruby twisted herself as far around as possible, she wanted to get face to face with him, but a searing pain in her left wrist made her cry out. She examined her wrist. The plastic tie had cut so deep that blood soaked into the sheets and mattress.

"Blood!" Kyle shuddered, his face screwed in disgust. Shaking his head, he put the fire engine underneath his arm and marched from the room, leaving the door open.

"Kyle!" Ruby screamed. "Kyle, please—I need you. It's an emergency."

Nothing. Her whole body trembled.

Think—think. There must be some way out. If she'd done what her mum insisted she do, there would probably be a search party arriving any minute. But all she'd told her mum was Cody's first name and the approximate location of the pub.

Taking another deep breath, she exhaled in a noisy blow and closed her eyes, bracing herself for one last try.

"Kyle?" she called, her voice now quieter—calmer. "I'd love to see your fire engine Kyle."

She heard the plastic rattle of the fire engine's wheels. Kyle was close by.

"It's okay, Kyle. There's no more blood. Why don't you come back in and I'll tell you about my uncle's fire engine?"

"It's-called-a-fire-TRUCK," Kyle said from somewhere outside the door.

"Oh, I'm sorry, buddy. My mistake—fire truck."

Kyle appeared in the doorway. Inching slowly forward, he held out the plastic red toy to show her.

"Wow! That's a beauty. Does it have a ladder?"

"Yup." Kyle's eyes lit up as he pointed to the ladder on the back of the truck.

"So it does," Ruby smiled. "And what about a fire hose?"

"Course-it-has-a-fire-hose-look." Kyle laughed. His blue eyes crinkling at the corners.

"My uncle told me that although they need the fire en ... truck, to put out the fires, a lot of their work is rescuing people from other situations."

Kyle's eyebrows furrowed.

"For example, they rescue a lot of cats from up trees."

"My-cat-climbs-trees."

"Does he? They also rescue people that are stuck."

"Up. Trees?"

Ruby laughed. "If someone climbs a tree and gets stuck, then yes, they'd rescue them. They would use the fire truck and cherry picker on top."

"Ah."

"But if a fire officer was here right now, he would rescue me by cutting these plastic ties and helping me get out of here."

Kyle backed up, shaking his head.

"No, Kyle—Kyle, come back, it's okay."

"I've-got-to-go. My-head-hurts."

"I'm sorry, Kyle. Just one more thing—do you know the number to call in an emergency?"

"Nine-nine-nine."

"Well done. Could I ask you to do it for me? Dial nine-nine-nine?"

"Kyle shook his head. "Not-an-mergency."

"It is. I'm trapped, see?"

Kyle scurried away.

"Kyle." Her voice was now tinged with hysteria.

The sound of tyres crunching on gravel filled the little room, followed by the slam of a car door and footsteps.

It was too late—she'd missed her opportunity to escape.

Steve kicked the door fully open, a frown on his face. He seemed relieved to see Ruby still tied to the bed. "Has somebody been here?"

Ruby shook her head, her lips tight shut. She didn't want to get Kyle into trouble.

"Who opened the door then?"

Ruby shrugged, whimpering.

Standing to the side of the bed, Steve checked her out from head to toe. The bulge in the crotch of his stonewashed jeans was unmistakable, even to her innocent eyes.

"Please Steve—I need to get home, Mum will be worrying by now."

"Oh no, she won't—Cody's seen to that."

"What do you mean?" she cried. The thought that Cody had hurt her mother tore at her insides.

Steve's laugh had a maniacal quality to it.

Ruby shuddered as she realised he was loony too.

He bent towards her face and inhaled deeply, as though he could smell her fear.

Ruby flinched and tried to twist away from him. Another searing pain in her wrist made her squeal.

"Look what you've done to yourself, silly girl," Steve said as he noticed the blood. He bent a little further and kissed the raw wound.

Ruby gasped for air, certain she was about to pass out if he didn't get out of her space. He didn't smell horrible. In fact, all Ruby could smell was polo mints, an aroma she normally loved as she associated it with her dad. But the sudden rush of nostalgia mixed with her current situation threatened to tip her over the edge.

Steve finally pulled back. He slid to his knees beside the bed, and with blood all over his lips and chin, he stroked her hair.

She whimpered. "Please, Steve, please …"

He leaned forward and his mouth muffled her screams.

Chapter 8

Cody dropped to his haunches. "Here, doggy-doggy," he said, holding his gloved fingers out towards the yapping pooch.

Eventually, the stupid dog came to investigate what Cody was offering and Cody punched it in the ribs with all his might. The dog yelped and raced from the room and up the stairs yelping all the way.

Cody chuckled before setting to work. He'd dropped Ruby's shoes in the hallway when he'd fallen. He now placed them side by side next to the door, as though somebody had just stepped out of them. He tapped the left one and it fell to the side. Cody smiled and nodded.

Taking the phone from his pocket, he brought up every text Ruby had sent and received from her sister, reading every one. Then he composed his own using the same tone and words Ruby would have used.

Hey, Scar. Just letting you know I'm home. Had a great night – c u tomoz, love Rubes xx

Cody had a quick look through the house, messing up the bed and closing the bedroom curtains. He placed Ruby's phone on the docking station and Amy Winehouse began singing *Rehab*.

He left the music playing while he made himself a slice of toast and cup of coffee, leaving the dirty cup and plate in the sink. He wanted to make sure it looked as though Ruby had come home alone.

Once satisfied, he placed the keys on the hall table and left via the back door. The typical *Yale* type lock didn't need a key to secure the door behind him.

In the small backyard, Cody climbed up onto the rubbish bin and over the top of the gate which had been bolted at the bottom. Whistling to himself, he strutted off down the back entry, to the end street where he found his car outside the shops. His dad had left his keys in the exhaust pipe as usual—something they always did.

Afterwards, feeling pleased with himself, he went round to Jed's bar which, despite the late hour, was just ramping up. Cody had been a regular there since moving to town as it was only a couple of blocks away from his flat.

He made a point of chatting to everyone he knew and after an hour or so, and two JD and cokes, he walked home.

Kenny Mac sat on the doorstep looking decidedly worse for wear.

"Hey Ken, What's up?"

"Oh, hey, Codes," Kenny slurred.

"Had a skinful have ya, mate?" Cody said, laughing.

"I've had the odd snifter here and there." He chuckled.

"Don't bother coming in if you're gonna throw up. I don't intend cleaning up after you again."

Kenny belched noisily.

"Fuck man, let me get in." Cody shoved his way into the hallway and ran up the stairs.

Kenny's girlfriend, Sam, and a girl Cody had never met before, were in the kitchen making pizza.

Cody bobbed his head into the lounge. Jez and Syd, Cody's flatmates, were with two other men. Jez was rolling a spliff.

"Hey guys," Cody said, before heading back to the kitchen. He made himself a coffee and listened to the two girls, who were obviously pissed off at Kenny. Sam's friend, a plain looking, dark haired girl, was encouraging Sam to dump his sorry arse.

Cody took his coffee and sat opposite them at the table. "Aren't you gonna introduce me to your friend, Sam?"

"Yeah, sorry. This is Kath. Kath—Cody."

"Hi Cody," Kath said, her voice suddenly taking on a sweet, girly tone.

Cody made a blatant play for her. She wasn't his cup of tea really, but after spending the evening with Ruby, his cock was straining against the fabric of his jocks. And besides, what better alibi was there than a girl getting rogered in his bed all night.

It didn't take long before he had her hanging off his every word. When he got up to leave, she looked as though she might burst into tears.

"Oh well, think I'll crash. Nice to meet you, Kath. Maybe we could go out for a drink one night?"

"I'd love that," she panted.

As he reached the door, he nodded his head and indicated with his eyes she should follow him. Within minutes, he had the dirty bitch stripped to her flimsy pink underwear, and sucking his cock as though her life depended on it.

Chapter 9

Ruby gasped for breath as Steve pulled away, groaning.

"I'm sorry. You're just so beautiful."

Ruby spat into the air several times, trying to get the taste of him from her mouth.

"Don't be like that, sweetheart. Maybe you need something to relax you a little."

Steve left the room, returning moments later with a bottle of whisky. He glugged from the neck of the bottle before holding it out towards her, then he laughed. "Oh, I'm sorry, I forgot."

He poured some of the amber fluid into the lid of the bottle and, after placing the bottle on the floor by the bed, he grabbed Ruby's head and held the whisky to her lips.

Ruby tried to resist, clamping her lips tight together, but he poured anyway. Horrible, stinking whisky ran down her chin and chest, and when she protested, the fiery liquid made it into her mouth. Ruby choked.

She'd never been a drinker. The odd glass of cider was her limit. She'd never even tried hard liquor before and from the taste of it, couldn't understand why anybody drank it willingly.

Steve took another drink, sucking on the neck of the bottle like a baby sucks on a teat, ending with a satisfied, "Ahhhh." He handed it back towards her, "More?"

She shook her head.

"Suit yourself."

He allowed his eyes to travel up and down her body once again.

"Please, please—let me go," Ruby begged, totally exhausted.

"Shhh."

Steve flashed hard eyes towards her. His demeanour seemed different from earlier.

"I'm not going to hurt you, I want to love you." He ran a hand down her side, over her waist and hip, to her knee. Then he slowly lifted the hem of her dress and traced the outline of her underwear with his fingertips, sucking in air between pursed lips.

Ruby whimpered again as tears ran down her face. She held herself rigid. Silent prayers filled her head, wishing for someone or something to intervene.

Once again, Steve placed the bottle down. He leaned forwards and unfastened the top button of her dress exposing her small breasts encased in the simple lacy bra. He gasped. "You are totally perfect."

Reaching for the bottle, he took another swig. "I suggest you get some shut-eye, my dear. We both should." Steve got to his feet and produced a roll of tape from his jacket pocket. He tore off a strip.

Ruby tried to wriggle away as he bent forward again, but the struggle was useless.

He placed the tape firmly across her mouth.

A loud, inarticulate sound escaped her. She thought she might pass out as in her panic she struggled to breathe through her nose.

"Sorry, sweetie. It's not that I think anyone will hear you—you've seen there're no neighbours, but I need some sleep and I won't get that if you're wailing all night."

She made a louder, angrier protest, but he ignored her.

"Sleep tight, Ruby." He switched the light off and left, closing the door behind him.

Sobs ripped through her and made it even harder to take a deep breath.

How the hell did she get herself into this? She'd always been so careful. But Cody had seemed sweet and sensitive—his dad too. She couldn't have been more wrong.

Now Cody had gone to sort her mother out, so Steve said. What the hell was that all about? Her mother was her only hope. Ruby had been relying on her mother's over-the-top protectiveness to alert the police when she hadn't returned home. Now she wasn't so sure.

Shivering, she tried to use her knees to flick her dress back down, but she couldn't. She figured the cold was the least of her worries right now.

Chapter 10

Cody couldn't sleep. Kath snored softly beside him in his double bed, her head on his arm. He shuddered. She wasn't his type—much too forward and sexually aware for his liking. However, he planned to keep her around for the rest of the night and most of tomorrow if he got his way. So he needed to keep her sweet.

He eased his arm out from under her and swung his feet out of bed, sitting on the edge. He wanted to call his dad to make sure everything was okay, but most of all to make sure his father had managed to keep his hands off Ruby. However, he would have a job explaining a call to his father at 3am while a hot and wanton hussy lay in his bed. No—he needed to be patient.

He thought back to the first girl he took home to his father—a French back-packer called Simone. He met her on the beach after she'd hitchhiked to the Welsh coast from the channel tunnel. He'd convinced her to go home with him, offering her room and board for a few odd jobs. She never even flinched when she realised the jobs they required of her were of a sexual nature.

After one rampant night, she left without a word, leaving behind one of her bags in Cody's car.

Cody felt sorry for his dad, he hadn't got over his wife vanishing—none of them had. But he never left the house anymore, never walking any further than the car and back. He hated open spaces and consequently, had never met any other women in years. Bringing women home seemed the only solution.

After the French girl, they began advertising in magazines—room and board in return for chores. They got a number of girls that way—always turning the males away. They were never disappointed, until the girls got tired of the strange set-up, of course, and decided to leave.

They always left without a word in the middle of the night.

That's when they decided to find a girl to keep.

Felicity Crew had been perfect—she had a sweet innocence about her that he and his dad both liked. When he met her on the coast road, her car wouldn't start. The area was a notorious black spot for mobile phones and so convincing her to get into his car had been a doddle.

They'd already set up the room off the garage by then and managed to spend two wonderful nights with her, when suddenly, she vanished.

Cody blamed his dad for not fastening the ties tight enough. But the strange thing was Felicity never made it home. They spent night after night expecting the police to raid their place but nothing. Felicity's image remained all over town on billboards and in local newspapers—her disappearance a total mystery.

Ruby was only their second guest—he thought of them as guests, not victims. She would be treated well, like any other guest would be, the only difference being, she wasn't allowed to leave.

Why did women always leave?

"Come back to bed," Kath groaned, reaching for him.

"In a minute." He unhooked her hand from his arm and placed it back under the duvet. "Shhh, go to sleep," he whispered.

He took a cigarette out of the packet she'd left on the bedside table and lit it, taking a deep drag. The room was briefly illuminated in an orange glow. He didn't smoke all the time, just when he was stressed.

His mind raced. If he was going to pull this off, he needed to keep his cool.

Chapter 11

Ruby cried with relief when Steve arrived the next morning. She made urgent sounds as she writhed on the bed.

"Hey, hey," he said, placing a tray down on the floor. He tore the tape off her face in one fluid movement.

"I need the toilet!" she gasped.

"Oh shit! I didn't think about that," he said. "Hang on."

He left, reappearing moments later with a pair of scissors. "Now, if I release you, you're not going to try anything stupid, are you?"

"No! Please hurry, I need to pee."

"Alright, keep your hair on." He cut through the plastic ties and grasped Ruby's upper arm as she got to her feet. "Now the bathroom is inside the house and upstairs. If there's any funny business, I'll bring a bucket in here and that will be where you'll do your business from now on. Got it?"

"Got it," Ruby said, rubbing at her wrists.

He led her indoors. The house stank of burnt toast.

At the top of the stairs, Steve pointed to a door on the left. "Leave the door open. I'll wait here."

Ruby didn't care about the open door at that point, she just needed to empty her bladder.

No sooner had she finished wiping herself when Steve stepped into the room.

"Do you mind?" Ruby said, pulling her underwear up and straightening her dress.

"Come on." He seemed agitated.

"Can I wash my hands, please?"

"If you're quick."

Ruby scanned the bathroom, trying to find something she could palm and use as a weapon later, but squirty soap was the only thing on the sink. Her reflection startled her—streaks of black mascara were all down her face and her was hair wild and matted.

"Come on, come on," Steve said, an impatient tone to his voice. He grabbed her upper arm once again before she had chance to dry her hands.

In panic mode, not wanting to go back into the cold white room, she resisted and struggled, but was surprised by Steve's strength. She eventually allowed him to bundle her back down the stairs while she scoured every surface with her eyes looking for something she could use as a weapon. There was nothing.

She knew she needed to keep her wits about her if she had any chance of escape. Back in the hateful room, she once again pushed against Steve.

"Please, I can't bear to be tied up again, can't you just …?"

"No-can-do, I'm afraid, love. But I'll make a deal with you."

Trembling, Ruby nodded.

"If you promise to behave, I'll just tie one wrist while you eat your breakfast."

Ruby was willing to agree to almost anything in order to prevent being fastened down again. "Okay-–okay," she said, suddenly breathless.

He eased her down onto the mattress. "Hand," he said, picking up the chain and feeding a tie through it.

"Steve, I ..."

"Hand." He gripped her right hand and with deft fingers, managed to secure her in seconds. "Okidoke, my girl. Eat up." He lifted the tray onto the bed beside her.

She turned her head away, but not before she spotted the plate of yummy food. There was bacon, sausage, egg and mushrooms. Much to Ruby's disgust her stomach betrayed her with a loud growl. She was starving and the sausage did look delicious.

"Go on," Steve urged as he saw her take another quick glance at the plate.

She picked up the sausage with her fingers and bit. Wanting to hate it—to spit it back onto the plate, but she couldn't. It was the nicest sausage she'd ever tasted and she devoured the lot in a few bites.

"That-a-girl. Go on, eat up. Now while you're finishing that little lot, I'll get you a drink. Tea? Coffee?"

"Coffee."

"Sugar?"

"Just milk, please." Ruby eyed him as he left the room. She was puzzled by his treatment of her. Apart from the strange cuddle, Steve had been kind—caring even. Maybe all that would change once Cody returned.

After a few seconds, Ruby snatched up the fork and stuck it down the side of the plastic tie and twisted. The tie didn't budge except to dig into her sore wrist. She tried several times until she heard Steve's shuffling footsteps. She stabbed a rasher of bacon and held it to her mouth as he entered.

"One cup of coffee." He held a cup towards her.

Ruby placed the fork back onto the plate and took the cup from him. "Thanks."

She wished she could throw the hot liquid into his face like they did in the movies, but she couldn't wilfully injure another person, regardless of what he intended to do to her. And besides, there was still a chance she could talk him round, convince him to let her go.

They sat in silence as she drank, Steve beside her on the bed.

She emptied the last of the delicious coffee and handed him the cup.

"Finished?" He got to his feet and reached for her other wrist.

"No—not yet." She lifted her arm away and grabbed a triangle of toast off the plate.

He sat back down.

"You're a good cook." She smiled, trying her best to appear sweet and grateful. Despite the fact that she still had mascara down her cheeks and probably looked more like a lunatic.

"That's good. I like a girl with an appetite. Karen had a good appetite but never seemed to put on an ounce of weight."

"Karen—was that your wife?"

Steve sighed. "Yes, my beautiful wife."

"Cody told me what happened. That must have been terrible for you."

Steve focused on a fleck of white fluff on the sleeve of his navy-blue sweatshirt. "You have no idea. Not a day goes by I don't think about her."

"I can't begin to imagine what it felt like. The not knowing alone must be terrible."

He closed his eyes, taking a deep breath. "I loved her so much," he whispered.

Ruby picked up the fork and flicked the bacon off, before sliding it into the tied hand, hiding the handle under her arm. "I know you did," she said, softly. "What do you think happened to her?"

He shrugged and shook his head. "The last time I saw her was when I left to take Cody to school, he was only doing mornings at the time. Kyle came with us to give Karen a break. As she waved us off, I remember thinking how lovely she was in her bright pink blouse and blue jeans. When I got back, she'd gone."

Ruby gasped, encouraging Steve on.

"I didn't think much of it at the time—just thought she must have popped out for something. She kept her car in the garage." He glanced around. "This room actually. But I didn't think to check. When she didn't return by lunch time, I collected Cody from school and we drove around looking for her car. I thought she must have broken down somewhere." He glanced at Ruby. "You see, it wasn't like nowadays. Nobody owned mobile phones back then."

"No, of course."

"Anyway, when I didn't find her, I called into the police station to report her missing. It wasn't until I got back home I realised her car was in the garage all along. I panicked then—knew something awful had happened."

He rubbed his eyes.

"The police thought she'd left me—blamed me for being the reason she'd run away. They searched the house. What they thought they might find was anybody's guess, but they didn't find a thing. Karen had vanished with no money, no car and only the clothes she stood up in."

He pinched in between his eyebrows—his eyes shut tight as though in great pain.

"Are you okay, Steve?"

"Yes." He shook himself as though just realising where he was and glanced at his watch. "Have you seen the time, I'd best get cleaned up. Cody might be back soon."

Her stomach dropped.

He pulled a handful of plastic ties from his pocket.

"Please don't tie my other arm and legs. It's not as if I can go anywhere and I promise I won't make a sound."

He cocked his head to one side as he considered her question. "Are you sure I can trust you?"

"I swear—I won't try anything."

"Any funny business and that's it." He picked up the tray. "I'll be back shortly." He headed for the door, then stopped and turned back to face her, holding the tray towards her.

"I've finished thanks."

He nodded. "Fork, please."

Ruby gave him a worried smile. "Sorry." She pulled out the fork and placed it onto the tray.

That-a-girl," he said before leaving.

Chapter 12

Cody and Kath slept until eleven. After another wild sex session, he made her breakfast in bed. Nothing Jamie Oliver would write home about—just poached eggs on toast, but you'd have thought he laid the eggs himself by the way Kath carried on.

While he was in the kitchen Cody called Ruby's mobile leaving a message asking her to call him—mentioning their amazing date. Then he sent two text messages saying pretty much the same. He wanted to appear keen to whoever read them but not come across as a stalker.

He didn't have to wait long for a response. His phone began ringing halfway through breakfast. He apologised to Kath and left the bedroom. Once in the bathroom, he braced himself before answering.

"Ruby, thank God. I was beginning to think you were avoiding my calls." He laughed.

"Hello is this Cody?" the irate caller said.

"Yes—who are you?" The laughter suddenly dropped from his voice.

"I'm Ruby's mother, Sharon. Do you know where she is?"

"I'm sorry?"

"She's gone—Ruby—she's gone."

"Gone? What do you mean gone?"

"What do you think I mean? She's not here. She's vanished. What time did you drop her off at home?"

"It was late. After midnight, maybe."

"Did you spend the night?"

"No. I dropped her off at the door, thank you very much."

"Well, she's not here now."

"Hang on—I'll come over."

Cody raced back into the bedroom and grabbed his jacket and keys. "Sorry, babe, but I've got an emergency. Leave your phone number and I'll call you later." He kissed her upturned cheek.

"I could wait?"

"I might be a while, but suit yourself."

He descended the stairs in three leaps and ran out to his car. It wasn't there. He slapped the heel of his hand against his forehead. He'd left it outside the bar last night. He set off at a sprint to collect his car.

Ten minutes later, he parked his car outside Ruby's house and was greeted at the door by a younger version of Ruby. She had the same long brown hair and peach coloured skin.

"Hi, are you Cody?" the girl said, holding her hand out towards him. "I'm Scarlett—Ruby's sister."

"Has she turned up yet?" Cody asked.

"No—it's so strange. She never goes anywhere without her phone."

"Maybe she just forgot to pick it up. Have you checked around her friends?"

"Mum's calling them now. Come on in, she'll want to talk to you. But be warned, she trusts nobody." Scarlett raised her eyebrows comically.

Taking a deep breath, Cody followed Scarlett into the house.

A short, dark-haired woman had her back to them as they entered the lounge. She had a phone to her ear.

"I'll have to go, Melissa. Let me know if you hear from her ... I will do, thanks, love."

The woman turned. "Ah, you must be Cody."

Cody nodded, his throat suddenly bone dry, and he couldn't swallow. He could feel his Adam's apple jumping in his throat.

"I'm Sharon, we spoke on the phone. Come in, sit down."

He sat on the lounge chair and Sharon perched on the arm of the sofa. Scarlett still hovered in the doorway.

"Scar—can you let Baxter in. I put him in the backyard to do his business," Sharon said.

Scarlett left. Sharon turned to him and in hushed tones said, "I'm worried, Cody. I've called the police and they said they'd send someone round. They didn't seem too concerned, but I am. I know my daughter and this just isn't like her."

"Could she be off visiting a friend?"

"No. I've called all her friends, and anyway, she knew we were coming. We walk to the market on a Saturday together—we've done it for years." She rubbed at her face and eyes. "Tell me, son. What happened last night?"

Cody instinctively knew what she meant. Although he didn't have black eyes as he'd expected, there was a small split on the bridge of his nose and slight bruising under his left eye.

"We went to a bar, and some guy decided he didn't like the look of me. He attacked me as we were leaving."

"Who was he?"

"Who?"

"The one who attacked you—who was he? Could he have followed you back here?"

Cody thought about it. "It's possible I guess, but why would he?"

"Why does anybody do anything? I've spoken to the neighbours. The woman across the road saw you drop her off. She knows the exact time was twenty past midnight—she wrote it down because she intended to report you for being a nuisance, sounding your horn so late."

"I didn't realise how late it was, I'm sorry."

"The elderly gentleman next door heard music playing into the early hours. Nobody saw her leave this morning."

Scarlett appeared with the little dog in her arms. It began snarling at him.

Scarlett laughed. "Hey, Baxy—you being a guard dog?"

"Cute dog," Cody said, getting to his feet.

"I know—but he was petrified when we found him this morning—he'd even pooed and peed under Ruby's bed, she'll be furious when she gets home."

Cody reached out to stroke the dogs head, but it flinched, it's snarls turning to whimpers.

Scarlett jumped back, holding the dog at arm's length. "The dirty bugger's just peed on me!" she squealed, and ran from the room.

Sharon's eyebrows furrowed as she looked back at Cody. Hairs prickled at the back of his neck.

"Okay, back to last night," she said. "If you don't know who the man was maybe someone at the pub will know him. Could you ask them?"

"I could. I don't know if anybody saw it though, we were already outside."

"Could you ask anyway? You never know."

"Okay. Give me two ticks."

Cody went outside and sat in his car. He felt jittery. He'd not expected Ruby's mum to unnerve him so much. She had a way of looking at him that made him feel she could see right through his lies. His instincts were to leave. Get out of there as fast as his legs could carry him, but that would alert them of a problem. He wasn't stupid, he just needed to pull himself together.

Back inside he found Scarlett and Sharon in the kitchen.

"Any luck?" Sharon asked.

"No—but they said they have cameras in the bar so maybe I can pick out the guy from the footage. I'm heading over there now. You've got my number so let me know if there's any change. I'll get back here as soon as I can."

Cody couldn't get out of there fast enough. He put his foot down once he was out of the town centre and sped towards the coast. He intended to call into his dad's house after the pub to check how things were there.

The bar staff were more than helpful. They recognised the thug immediately and even supplied his name and approximate address. They'd been watching him for a while.

All seemed normal as he parked his car outside the house. Surprised to find Ruby's door slightly ajar, he tapped it open with his boot.

Ruby jumped to her feet.

"Who untied you?" Cody shouted.

"No-one—I'm not untied." She indicated her right wrist.

"You know what I mean."

"What did you do to my mum?" she asked.

"What the fuck you on about?"

"Your dad said you'd gone to sort out my mum."

Cody shook his head and sighed. "Where's Dad?"

"Tell me you didn't hurt her."

"I didn't fucking hurt her—what do you think I am? A monster?"

He went in search of his father.

"Dad?" He slammed through the front door.

His father appeared in the kitchen doorway. "Hi, son. How'd you get on?"

Cody shrugged. "Why's she not tied up? Did you learn nothing from last time?"

"She is tied up. She's just had a sandwich for lunch and a bathroom visit."

"You need to make sure she's tied up at all times."

"Alright, son. Keep your hair on."

"Codee," Kyle said, rushing into the kitchen. "Did-you-get-it?"

"Get what?"

"My-new-fire-truck."

"No—sorry dude, I forgot." Cody ruffled Kyle's shaggy blond hair.

"But-I-beened-good."

"I know, Kyle. Next time, I promise."

Kyle left the room his shoulders sagging and moments later music blared from his bedroom.

"So tell me. What's happening?" his dad said.

"It's all sweet. Her mother's a bit of a battle axe, but she doesn't suspect me. In fact, she thinks Ruby's disappearance might have something to do with the dick'ead from the pub last night." Cody smiled, pleased with himself.

"Now, if you don't mind, I'll tie her up before another one gets away. Have you forgotten how you felt when Felicity escaped? Watching the clock, wondering how long it would be before she turned up and we were arrested?"

"Of course I haven't forgotten, but she's alright. We've had a chat."

Cody shook his head, exasperated. "You really don't get it, do you? She's not your girlfriend. She's not even your friend. First chance she gets, she'll be out that door and we'll be behind bars. Is that what you want?" Cody yelled. He needed to get it through his dad's fucking thick head. If this turned to shit it would be Cody's neck on the block, nobody else's.

"No Cody, it isn't."

"Then do as I say. Tie her securely at all times—tape her mouth if you leave her for any length of time. Got it?"

"Got it."

Cody shoved his dad aside and headed back to Ruby.

When Cody burst back into the little room, Ruby squealed and scrambled backwards on the mattress until her back was up against the wall.

"Okay, Ruby. Lie yourself down for me, sweetheart."

"Please, Cody, no. I promise I'll …"

"Not negotiable, I'm afraid. Now do as you're told," he bellowed.

"No, I'm begging you."

Sick and tired of being ignored, Cody grabbed Ruby's foot and yanked her backwards. He wasn't prepared for the sickening crunch as her head connected with the edge of the makeshift steel headboard he'd used to secure the bed to the wall.

Ruby screamed as blood gushed from the back of her head.

"What the fuck have you done to her?" his dad said, falling to his knees beside the bed.

"I didn't do anything. She banged her head, that's all."

"You banged her head, Cody. You," his dad hissed.

"Whatever. Get her cleaned up and fastened securely before I get back. I don't have time for this."

Chapter 13

Cody was relieved to get out of there. Ruby was crying and bleeding all over the place. Stupid bitch. He didn't even do anything. It wasn't his fault she whacked her head. If she'd been tied properly in the first place, none of this would have happened. But as usual, his dad changed the rules. Allowing himself to be coerced and manipulated by a pretty face and a decent pair of tits. That fucking Ruby was taking liberties—she deserved all she got.

He drove at breakneck speed on along the country roads, once again, forcing himself to slow down as he approached the town.

A police car was parked outside Ruby's house.

Cody sat in the car gripping the steering wheel until he had the courage to go inside.

The door opened as he approached and Scarlett stepped backwards allowing him to enter. "Any luck?" she asked.

"Yes, actually."

"Come through, Cody," Sharon called from the lounge.

The two police officers, one a plain looking woman in her twenties and the other, a square-shaped middle-aged man, sat side by side on the sofa. Both got to their feet when he entered.

Cody noticed the stupid little dog lying on a mat beside the hearth. It started growling when he spotted Cody and it's entire body began to quiver. Cody tried to ignore him.

"This is Cody, the one I was telling you about," Sharon informed the officers. "Sorry Cody, I don't know your surname ..."

"Strong. Cody Strong."

The officers nodded at Cody before sitting back down.

"Thanks," Sharon continued. "Cody was the last person to see Ruby in the early hours of this morning."

"We believe there was an altercation last night," the female officer said. "Did you manage to find out the name of the man who attacked you?"

"I did, yes. His name's Peter Cross. Apparently he lives on the Mayor Estate."

She scribbled something onto a pad. "Where do you live, Mr Strong?"

"Twenty-two Fernleigh Street. I share a flat with two others."

"And can you tell me what time you left Ruby and where you went afterwards?"

"Of course. Apparently the neighbour knows the exact time I dropped her off. Then I went to Jed's bar."

"Can anybody confirm this?"

"Why are you asking me this? Do you think I had something to do with her going missing?"

"We just need to establish your whereabouts at this stage, sir. Nothing for you to worry about," the male officer said, in a hoarse gravelly voice.

"Well, I saw a few friends—Roger Bell from the butchers on the high street, and Joan Davies, the barmaid. There were others too."

"That should be enough for now. How long did you stay there?" the female officer asked.

"An hour or so. Not long really."

"And then what did you do?"

"Went home. My flatmates can vouch for me. I didn't go out again after that."

"Okay, thank you, sir."

She turned back to Sharon.

"We'll make some enquiries, but at this stage I'd say there's nothing to worry about. I'm sure she'll show up before too long."

"No—you're wrong. Something's happened to her—I know—I know it …"

"There's no sign of a struggle or a break in. Nobody saw or heard anything. The house was all locked up."

"Yes—but her keys are still here."

"Maybe she had a spare," the policeman said.

"I took her only spare—plus her phone is still here. Honestly, she never goes anywhere without it."

The female officer got to her feet. "Leave it with us. We'll check out this Peter Cross character and get back to you shortly. In the meantime, if she should show up, please let us know right away."

The policeman stood up and turned back to Cody. "Cody Strong … you're not related to Steven Strong by any chance are you?"

"Yes. He's my dad."

"Ah, so it was your mother who vanished from her home up near Melody Falls years ago?"

"Yes, that's right." Cody struggled to maintain an even tone while he could hear his heartbeat thumping in his ears.

"Where's your dad living these days?"

"Same place—he's never moved."

"Still up on the hill there? A bit too remote for me, but a stunning spot. Tell him Officer Croydon said hi."

He clapped Cody roughly on the back.

They left, and Cody thought he might vomit with relief. He'd never been so nervous in the whole of his life.

After seeing the officers out, Scarlett came back into the lounge and sat on the carpet beside her mum. "So what now?"

"Why won't they take me seriously? I have a bad feeling about this." Sharon poked at the inside corners of her eyes.

"They will, Mum. They just need to wait a little longer."

"At least Cody got that guy's details. Let's hope they pay him a visit right away."

"Shall I make us all a coffee?" Cody asked, feeling claustrophobic in the tiny room.

"Thanks, that'll be nice." Sharon smiled, her eyes were full of unshed tears.

Cody reached the door when Scarlett cried, "Baxter! What the hell's the matter with you?" Cody almost jumped out of his skin at the raised voice. His nerves were frazzled. He shot out of the room. The conversation followed him down the hallway.

"Look, Mum. He's peed again—in his bed this time."

"Put him outside. I've got enough on my mind without having to worry about a dirty, bloody dog," Sharon said.

In the kitchen, Cody busied himself making coffee. Scarlett eased past him, holding the dog at arm's length and threw it into the yard.

"Ruby keeps her coffee in the tea canister in the cupboard," she said.

"Thanks—I found it."

"Did you? It took me half an hour to find it this morning and I only found it in the end when I decided to have tea instead." She laughed.

Shit! Cody thought. He'd also spent ages the night before trying to find the coffee. If he wasn't careful, they would be questioning if he had actually been inside the house before today.

Scarlett didn't seem in the least suspicious. She prattled on about instant coffee being just as good as real coffee.

He nodded, agreeing with her completely.

Scarlett took her mug from him and Cody carried the other two mugs through to the lounge.

"Thanks, sweetheart," Sharon said as he handed one to her.

"Oh, hang on. What's that on your cheek? Is it blood?"

Cody froze.

Sharon rubbed a thumb across his cheek. "It is blood!"

"I had another nosebleed earlier," he said. "I haven't had a nosebleed since I was a kid, that guy must have caused some damage."

"You'd better get it checked out," she said.

He gave an internal sigh. Fuck, this was getting too close for comfort.

Cody spent the rest of the day there. Eating chocolate chip cookies and drinking copious amounts of coffee.

The police finally returned just as it was going dark.

The female officer took the lead once again. "We've ruled out Peter Cross. He's a nasty piece of work, just as you described, Mr Strong. But after assaulting you, he was arrested for assaulting another young man. He spent the night in a cell."

"We've also checked your alibi and they all confirm your version of events."

"Someone called Kath is still waiting at your flat," the male officer said, raising one eyebrow at Cody.

Cody was relieved they didn't say any more in front of Sharon.

Once the police had left, Cody also left for home, promising to return at first light if Ruby still hadn't shown up.

He practically skipped to his car.

Chapter 14

The blow to her head caused Ruby to fade in and out of consciousness.

She was vaguely aware of Steve bathing the wound at one point. And another time Kyle played with his fire engine on the floor beside the bed.

It seemed much later when she came around again as the light was fading and the temperature had dropped.

Startled by a sound to the side of her, Ruby turned to find Kyle dressed in a fireman's outfit including a shiny helmet.

"Hello, Fireman Kyle," Ruby said.

"I-come-to-rescue-you."

"Thank you, Kyle." Ruby began fading again.

When she regained consciousness, cold air hit her face and she realised she was upright. Kyle half-carried and half- dragged her through the garden, her bare feet skimming the ground.

"KYLE!" Steve yelled from somewhere close behind them.

"Kyle—you come back here this minute."

"Can't. It's-a-mergency."

Ruby tried to move her legs to help Kyle, but she couldn't. However, he seemed strong enough to keep going at speed.

"Kyle!" Steve yelled again.

Ruby didn't know where the garden ended and the dense forest began, but Kyle didn't seem perturbed—he just sped on regardless.

"Kyle!"

Ruby couldn't understand why Steve didn't seem to be following them. His voice was getting fainter the further they went. She still felt woozy and sleepy, but she forced herself to stay awake. Stray twigs and branches dug into her arms and legs as they rushed between the trees.

"Where are you taking me, Kyle?"

"Safe-place."

Ruby was too exhausted to say anything more.

They eventually came to a clearing and as far as Ruby could tell, a dead end. A steep rock wall surrounded them on three sides, the only way out was back the way they came.

Kyle eased Ruby down onto a fallen tree branch. "Wait-here."

Ruby watched as Kyle produced a key from his jacket pocket and then began pulling at the dense ivy that scaled the rock wall.

Suddenly the green growth came away with a loud snap, unveiling an old gate covering a tunnel into the rock. She remembered Cody telling her the land used to belong to a mining company.

Kyle fiddled with the lock and the gate creaked part way open. "Safe-place." Kyle pointed inside the tunnel.

He helped her to her feet and eased her towards the opening.

"I can't go in there, Kyle!" she squealed.

"Safe-place. Goes-to-river."

"I can't—I'm scared of the dark."

"It's-a-mergency." He nodded, urging her through the gate.

Ruby gripped at one of his hands and looked him in the eyes. "Please Kyle, I'm scared."

"Safe-place. River."

"Can't I get to the river another way?"

"No-it's-rock." He slammed the flat of his hand onto the granite above her head, in case she was in any doubt it was real. "Safe-place. Promise." He unpeeled her fingers from his hand and pushed her inside, closing the gate behind her. She cried hysterically as he replaced the padlock and pulled the ivy back into place taking the last of the light.

"Kyle, please let me out," she called.

"Safe-place. Kyle-rescue-you."

Then she heard his footsteps trudge away.

Petrified and light headed, Ruby staggered a few feet until in total darkness. She began to feel her way.

The further she went, the narrower the tunnel became. Eventually, she slid to her knees and crawled. Her head thudded and her eyes grew heavy.

She gave in to the darkness.

Chapter 15

The cold dank air hit her nostrils like a sledgehammer. Ruby recoiled. Froze. Held her breath. After a few minutes, she tried to turn her head, but immense pain shot through her temples, settling to a dull throb at the base of her skull. She fought to keep her eyes open, needing to remember where the hell she was. She couldn't. She gave in to the heavy, drifting sensation.

Not sure how much time had passed, she reached up to touch the tender spot on the back of her head. A cry escaped her as a thick stickiness came away on her fingertips. The metallic scent of blood now mingled with the earthy wet stench surrounding her.

She shivered uncontrollably as blood gushed through her veins in unison with the thudding inside her head.

She could see nothing. Not a thing.

Were her eyes even open?

She knew they were when she felt them close once again.

The only sound was the continuous drip-drip-drip that came from all around her.

She managed to roll onto her back. Icy rock almost touched her on either side. She reached up and yelped as the tips of her fingers hit more hard rock not six inches above her face.

She was in a tunnel—a cold, dark, terrifying tunnel.

Ruby was disoriented. She crawled forward in the direction she faced.

Memories began flooding her mind. Cody, Steve and Kyle. A sob caught in her throat.

Her back scraped on the jutting rock as she manoeuvered her way forward. Her head connected with sharp rock and she cried out. The impact made her sink her teeth into her tongue. Now blood filled her mouth.

Kyle had seemed certain this awful tunnel led to the river. The sound of water became louder and more of a steady flow rather than a drip. Ruby prayed the end was close by.

A small, furry creature ran across her hand, squeaking. She screamed, her head once again banging on the rock.

Her teeth chattered.

All her fears surrounded her.

Enclosed spaces—scurrying creatures—bone crippling cold.

She sensed a change to her surroundings when a draught blew on her face.

Sobbing now, she pushed forward. Small slivers of light enabled her to see in front of her and she gasped as she stepped out into a cave-like clearing. Climbing down from the rock, Ruby stood full height. She headed off in the direction of the light.

All of a sudden, a large opening appeared and the early morning sky beyond.

On weak and shaky legs she forced herself on, her eyes filled with tears making the opening appear blurred. Then she suddenly realised it had nothing to do with the tears.

A cry caught in her throat.

Her legs propelled her forwards.

A padlocked wrought iron gate covered the entire opening.

But that wasn't the worst of it.

The remains of a woman wearing a multi-coloured jersey were slumped to the side of the gate, the bones of her hands still gripping the bars.

Ruby's screams filled the silence.

Chapter 16

Ruby slid to the ground—exhausted from screaming. Although unable to look at poor Felicity's corpse any longer, every time she closed her eyes it was all she could see, in intricate detail. She kept getting flashes of the news image—a vibrant, fun-loving young girl wearing the same multi-coloured jersey that covered the skeleton beside her.

Her neck and the back of her dress felt wet. She knew she was losing her life's blood, she could feel the last of her strength oozing away. She prayed the end would be fast. Ruby welcomed the heavy darkness.

When she came to, her whole body shivered. Her teeth were chattering and she could see puffs of her shallow breath hovering on the air in front of her face.

Through the gate she could see the sun beating down, but it came nowhere near the cave which was deep in shadow.

She dragged herself further into the cave in search of some warmth. A few feet in and off to the right, she came across a pile of rocks, all different sizes, placed in a large rectangle shape. It reminded Ruby of a grave. She shuddered, wishing she could run from this place of death, but she couldn't move another inch. Resting her head on her arm, she floated off once again.

The light had faded when she finally woke. The temperature had dropped even more—she might as well have been naked for all the warmth the wispy summer dress gave her.

From her position next to the grave-like mound, she could see something colourful lodged between two rocks. She picked at it until she finally managed to pry it out. It was a small white card with a spray of pink roses, barely visible, printed on one side.

Ruby's blood froze in her veins—a bereavement card. Not really wanting to know what it said, but intrigued, she turned the card over. She could see an imprint of handwriting, but no ink remained and in the failing light, she had no chance of reading what had once been written. She carefully placed it back between the rocks.

She shuffled down the side of the grave-like mound and curled herself into a foetal position, pulling the fine dress tight around her knees. She then pulled her arms from the sleeve openings and hugged her body tightly.

Her stomach growled. Although she hadn't had a thing to eat or drink since the day before she no longer felt hungry or thirsty. She didn't feel that cold thinking about it now, for which she was grateful. There was no way out. She knew she would die soon, but if she couldn't feel the pain, at least she could sleep.

Ruby stayed in that position for what seemed like hours. She drifted in and out of sleep, or consciousness, she couldn't really tell.

She wished she had the energy to go back to the gate and try to force it open somehow, but she wasn't able to move a muscle. Maybe she should have gone back through the tunnel earlier when she hadn't felt as bad, but she'd seen

Kyle secure the padlock with her own eyes. The idea of crawling back through that awful tunnel, or worse, dying in there, made her flesh crawl.

Her head began to throb again and her limbs felt heavy and weak. She couldn't keep her eyes open.

Her mother's constant warnings filled her fitful dreams. Then Baxter's barks made her heart contract. Semi-awake, she panicked. Baxter! What if he hadn't been found? If he was still locked in her house, alone?

Oh, Baxy, Baxy. I'm sorry, boy. She wasn't sure if she'd actually spoken the words or dreamt them. Baxter's excited yaps were louder now, almost deafening. She could actually feel him licking her face. It seemed so real, she didn't want to wake up. She relished in the heat his tiny body radiated. His excited yappy kisses were forcing her awake, but still she resisted. Holding her breath, she forced her eyes tight shut.

"Baxter?" someone yelled, spoiling her dream.

Baxter was gone and she heard herself whimper not wanting the dream to end. Her heart ached at the thought of opening her eyes to the cold, dark cave.

"Baxter—come here, boy."

There was that voice again. She recognised it, but for the life of her, couldn't think who it was.

Ruby felt herself slipping away once more. With Baxter no longer with her, she welcomed the familiar heaviness.

"Baxy, where is she, boy?"

Who *was* that? And why was he calling Baxter?

Suddenly Baxter returned, licking at her face.

"Baxy, good boy, Baxy," she managed to utter.

"Ruby?" The voice, now closer, echoed off every wall. "Ruby, Ruby—wake up."

She tried to open her eyes, but they were much too heavy. Then she heard footsteps and Baxter began barking again. She felt herself being lifted into someone's arms, and suddenly recognised the voice. It was David. Her ex-boyfriend—her mum's next door neighbour.

"David?" she whispered.

"Yes, you're safe now, Rubes. Try not to speak—save your energy."

She couldn't understand how her dreams could feel so real. Had she died? If she had, why would David be there? It was all too confusing.

Epilogue

Ruby forced her eyes open and a cry caught in her throat. The cold, dark cave had been replaced by a hospital bed.

Her beautiful mother slept in an armchair to her side, her bottom lip inflating with every breath before letting out a pffft of air. Ruby was overjoyed, although much too tired to react.

A middle-aged woman with both legs in casts lay in the bed opposite. She poked a pen into the top of one cast, clearly trying to reach an itch.

So she hadn't been dreaming. Baxter and David had found her—but how? She needed to know, but after a sleep.

David, Scarlett and her mother were around the bed when Ruby opened her eyes again.

Scarlett squealed and jumped forward, hugging her neck, and after the initial tears and emotional reunion, Mum and Scarlett began chattering in unison.

Ruby winced. "Shhhh. Please guys, one at a time." Her head still felt woozy.

"You go," her mother said to Scarlett, tears still streaming down her face.

"How?" Ruby asked.

"Mum worked everything out, sis. She could tell Cody was bad news as soon as she laid eyes on him. I didn't. I thought he was lovely." Scarlett shook her head. "I'll never doubt her instincts again, I can tell you ..."

"But how did you find me?"

"David followed Cody. Once we found out where he lived we all turned up. David was ace! He didn't take any shit from Cody or his dad."

"Thank you," Ruby mouthed at David.

David winked at her and smiled—the special smile he used to reserve only for her.

Ruby's stomach flipped.

"Kyle was lovely. He showed us where he took you," Scarlett continued.

"Felicity?" Ruby asked, her voice hoarse.

"She's back where she belongs—with her family," her mother said. "At least now they can give her a proper funeral."

"And the other grave?" Ruby asked.

"Cody's mum," Scarlett said. "Seems she was going to leave her husband and so he strangled her. He used to take Kyle to visit there, that's how Kyle knew about the old mine in the first place."

"They always went by car, approaching from the other side. Kyle didn't remember there being a gate, but he was only little. Then years later, his dad took him and Cody into the mine entrance closest to the house. He told them the tunnel led through to the river. Kyle worked the rest out for himself," David said.

"What will happen to them?"

"Cody and his dad will be locked up for the foreseeable I guess," David said.

"And Kyle?"

Mum shrugged. "He's in good hands Rubes. He'll be taken care of, and you can always visit him."

"How did you work it out, Mum?"

"Fifty percent instinct. Then Baxter, the dog who loves everyone, was petrified of Cody—combined with the fact his mother had vanished but he didn't even think to mention it to us. I saw blood on his face ... lots of little things really. But the police had verified his alibi and so we had no choice but to deal with it ourselves."

"Wow, I can't believe it."

"Believe it. I've told you many times—"

"We know, we know," Scarlett said.

"Mother knows best!" they all chanted in unison.

ABOUT THE AUTHOR

Netta Newbound, originally from Manchester, England, now lives in New Zealand with her husband, Paul and their boxer dog Alfie. She has three grown-up children and two delicious grandchildren.

For more information or just to touch base with Netta you will find her at:
www.nettanewbound.com
Facebook
Twitter

Acknowledgements

Massive hugs go to my family—especially my long suffering husband, Paul—love you, babe!

To my wonderful critique partners Sandra Toornstra, Linda Dawley, Serena Amadis and Jono Newbound—you're the best.

And finally, to the BOCHOK Babes – my go-to group for anything from critiquing to formatting or just a good old moan. Where would I be without you?

An Impossible Dilemma by Netta Newbound

Local vets Victoria and Jonathan Lyons seem to have everything—a perfect marriage, a beautiful five-year-old daughter, Emily, and a successful business. Until they discover Emily has a rare and fatal illness.

Early trials show that a temporary fix would be to transplant a hormone from a living donor. However in the trials; the donors had died within twenty four hours. They have no choice but to accept their daughter is going to die.

When Jonathan is suddenly killed in a farming accident, Victoria turns to her sick father-in-law, Frank, for help. A series of events present Victoria and Frank with a situation that, although illegal, could help save Emily.

Will they take it?

Sample chapter to follow …

Chapter 1

"She looks terrible, Jon. We should have taken her straight to the hospital."

The shrill peal of the surgery phone made my stomach twirl. I spun around as Stacey, the pretty, young blonde receptionist lifted the receiver, her voice all sickly sweetness.

I glanced around the room. Apart from an elderly gentleman dozing in the corner, we were the only people waiting to see the doctor. The clinic had had a makeover since my last visit—the pale cream walls, glossy magazines, and plush maroon covers on the chairs presented the image of an upmarket clinic instead of the laid-back, sleepy practice we knew it to be.

"Stop being a fusspot, Victoria. We're here now." Jonathan stroked Emily's forehead. She lay half on his knee with her legs sprawled out on the bench seat beside him. He pinched her chin and smiled down at her. "Mummy's being a fusspot, isn't she, Miss Em?"

Emily nodded, her large grey eyes rolling as he stroked her golden brown curls.

"You know he's going to say she has a virus or some other rubbish. The hospital would at least do tests," I said, stopping mid-pace in front of them.

Jon reached for my hand and pulled me down beside him. "I get that you're worried, Vic. We both are. And if things are no clearer after we've seen the doc, we'll go straight to the hospital."

"You promise?"

"I promise."

I bent to kiss the top of my daughter's head. Her eyelids fluttered and closed again.

As I sat up, I noticed Stacey gazing at us with interest. The village nosy parker was probably looking for a story to keep her friends entertained. Our eyes met, and she quickly turned away.

I chewed at the inside of my cheek, a habit I'd formed when in stressful situations as a child. It would be sore later.

At the sound of a buzzer, we both turned towards Stacey, who got to her feet and nodded at the old man. "You can go through now, Mr Delaney."

All of a sudden, I thought I was going to vomit. I needed to get out. "I'm going for some fresh air. Give me a shout when it's our turn," I said, kissing

Emily once more before heading for the double doors.

Outside, the chilly afternoon wind took my breath. I sat on the cold, stone surgery steps, pulled my orange woollen jumper over my knees, and hugged my legs. Daffodils filled the two garden squares on either side of the steps.

I sighed as the familiar hollow ache resurfaced between my ribs. Memories of my mother's daffodil-laden casket brought tears to my eyes. I missed her so much. My fingers closed around her gold locket that I wore on a chain around my neck.

My legs began to bounce with irritation; the long wait had my nerves at screaming point. One of the problems with living in the country was the slow pace of village life. We'd been here almost six years, and I was still trying to acclimatise.

I was used to large surgeries with umpteen doctors to choose from. Here you got who were given, like it or lump it.

We'd sold our veterinary clinic in Manchester after Frank, Jon's father, had suffered a stroke. Jon was an only child, and the responsibilities of the farm fell solely at his size nines.

Jonathan had been born on the farm, and Doctor Taylor, our family doctor, had even delivered him—as he had most of the children in the area. But Doctor Taylor had gone to New Zealand for a year, leaving a locum in his place.

A hammering on the window behind me jolted me from my daydream. Jonathan was standing behind the glass, waving at me to hurry.

Doctor Davies seemed too young to be fully qualified. He had a large moon-shaped face with a helmet of floppy, fine blond hair atop a head that looked too big for his weedy body.

"Hello—this must be Emily," the doctor said with an overused, insincere smile.

"Hello," Emily whispered.

"Are you feeling poorly, sweetheart?"

I inhaled noisily and raised my eyes to the wooden panelled ceiling before refocusing on Jon.

Jonathan's eyes flashed at me as he gave his head a tight shake.

I shrugged and turned away, fiddling with the locket at my throat.

Emily nodded and closed her eyes, leaning against Jon's shoulder again.

"She's not been right for a while, doctor. She's lethargic and clumsy. I don't know—just off, somehow," Jonathan said.

The doctor nodded, raised his eyebrows and began typing on a keyboard in front of him.

"I've been doing some research and I'm positive she has some kind of neurological disorder," I said.

Doctor Davies stopped typing and took off his frameless glasses. His beady brown eyes locked on mine. "Are you a doctor, Mrs—," he glanced at the computer screen, "—Lyons?"

"A vet. I'm a vet—we're vets," I wiggled a finger between Jon and myself. "And although I'm not a doctor—doctor, I know my stuff, *and* I know my daughter."

The doctor cleared his throat and sighed. His hands were in a praying position in front of his face, the index fingers touching the tip of his nose, contemplating me.

"I'm sure you do, Mrs Lyons, but let's go through this from the beginning for my benefit, shall we? Then I will try to make my own diagnosis, and we can compare notes later. Is that okay with you?" he said.

His patronizing attitude was starting to get my back up. I bit my lip and stifled a sigh, trying to eyeball Jonathan, who did his best to avoid my stare. Of course the doctor needed to make his own diagnosis, but I didn't want him poo-pooing Em's symptoms and just throwing a course of antibiotics at her.

"It started a few months ago," I said.

"Months?" the doctor's eyebrows furrowed.

"Yeah, but nothing bad. Just subtle changes at first. Jonathan blamed the clumsiness on her age."

"Typical five-year-old, doc," Jon said. "Too impatient to get where she wants to go. She climbs over anything in her path. I thought her falls were nothing more than that."

The doctor nodded. "So what changed?"

"This weekend, her coordination deteriorated. She struggled to feed herself and she was so clumsy she could fall over her own feet from standing still." I bent forward and stroked Emily's face.

"That's why we made an appointment first thing this morning." Jon said.

I nodded. "She slept most of the day, but by this afternoon, when I tried to wake her up, her speech had become slurred. She sounded drunk. Obviously I panicked and rang Jonathan, insisting he come home immediately. I wanted to take her straight to the hospital, but he said we should keep the appointment."

"Do you want to pop Emily onto the table and let me have a quick look at her?" He indicated the examination table in a curtained-off area at the side of the room.

Jonathan carried Emily to the table and tried to lie her down, but she held her body stiff and refused to cooperate.

"Filly, I want Filly," she cried.

"Shit," I said, looking around. "Where's Filly, Jon?"

"At home?" He shrugged.

"No, she had her in the truck."

"She must still be in the truck, then."

"I'll check," I said. "Emily, let the nice doctor have a look at you and I'll go and get Filly for you. Okay?"

She nodded, her eyes closing again as Jonathan managed to lie her down.

I suddenly noticed Jon's face had lost all colour and his normally vibrant grey eyes were dark with black smudges beneath them.

As I stepped through the double doors, a loud crash rang out from the back of the surgery, immediately followed by a car alarm.

I raced down the steps and along the side of the old brick building.

The door to Jonathan's truck stood open, and a man was leaning inside.

I stopped mid-stride. My insides dropped as my hand flew to my mouth. The outrage of this person stealing our belongings propelled me forward.

I grabbed the collar of his red and black checked lumberjack shirt and yanked him backwards.

"Hey!" he yelled, as he found himself flat on his back on the concrete.

I recognized him immediately.

"Well, well. Why am I not surprised? Shane Logan," I said.

He and his family were well known in the area. None of them had had any education, and probably had never done an honest day's work in their lives.

"Fuck off, bitch," he said. His lip lifted in a sneer, and hatred filled his eyes.

"You cheeky little—" Adrenalin coursed through me, exacerbated by all the pent-up anxiety of the past few weeks. A guttural roar escaped me as I smacked him around the head with the flat of my hand.

"Victoria. Stop!" Jonathan yelled as he appeared around the corner. Emily was wrapped around his neck, her pathetic little arms holding on for dear life as Jon ran across the car park towards us.

"Yes, Victoria. Stop," the scumbag mimicked like a child. He was still on the ground, one arm raised above his head as he cowered beneath it, trying to scuttle away from me.

Emily began to cry.

"Call the police, Jon. This piece of shit smashed your window and dismantled your stereo," I said, trying to control the urge to punch the cocky waste of space on his scruffy, ginger goatee. I dug my nails into my palms.

Emily sobbed. "Filly, I want Filly."

I reached into the back seat and plucked out the scruffy rag doll Emily carried everywhere. I threw it to Jonathan, and Emily snatched it from him and held it to her chest. Jonathan continued to bounce her on his hip and stroke her hair, trying to calm her down.

I turned back to the nasty creature at my feet. "Stand up!"

"Fuck off," he said with a sneer—or maybe it was his pathetic attempt at a smile.

"Watch your mouth, boy," Jonathan said, pulling Emily's head into his chest and covering her exposed ear.

"You fuck off too, dick'ead." Shane stood up and spun away from us.

"Come back here, Shane," I said.

"Up yours, MILF. You know—Mum I'd like to ..." He thrust his disgusting pelvis in my direction, his tongue sticking out of the corner of his mouth and his eyes rolling in mock ecstasy.

"Enough!" Jonathan stepped towards him. "Shift yourself now, Shane, before I kick your arse myself."

"OOO-ooh." Shane's eyebrows rose as he sneered at Jonathan. He sniffed noisily, then hoicked a large glob of spit on the ground at Jonathan's feet before sauntering off.

My stomach churned. "You dirty little ... Jonathan, call the police!" I said, approaching Shane.

Shane rounded the end of the truck then ran, pausing briefly to flip us the finger.

"Why would you just let him go?" I turned on my husband, fuming.

Jonathan had opened the boot of the car and threw a towel at me.

"Clear the glass from the seat while I fasten Emily in," he said, as though nothing had occurred.

His serious no-nonsense tone worried me. I stared at him, completely lost for words.

"I'll tell you when we get home."

"What did the doc ... ?"

He tipped his head towards our daughter, his eyebrows raised. "When we get home."

***

Once Emily was snuggled up on the sofa with her favourite fleecy pink blanket, watching a DVD, Jonathan nodded his head towards the kitchen.

I got up and followed him.

"Now can you tell me why you did that?" I was stalling, not yet ready for him to tell me what the doctor said that got him so worked up.

"Did what?" A puzzled expression crossed his face.

"Did what? Are you serious? He smashed your window, for Christ's sake. He'd have had your stereo and anything else he could get his thieving little mitts on if I hadn't stopped him." I couldn't believe he didn't seem to care. I shook my head, bewildered.

"Oh, that." He rubbed a hand over his chiselled, bristly jaw.

"Yes, that!" I said, exasperated.

"To be honest, Shane Logan is the least of our worries right now, Vic," he said, his eyes filled with concern.

"Why? What did the doctor say?" I braced myself for bad news. Spine-tingling dread began spreading through my entire body.

The kitchen door opened and Frank, Jonathan's father, shuffled in. He froze as he realised we were deep in conversation.

"Sorry, am I interrupting?" Frank said, and turned to leave.

"No, Dad, come in. You need to hear this too."

"Hear what?" I shivered as each tiny hair on the back of my neck stood to attention.

Frank closed the door and, leaning heavily on his stick, limped over to stand beside his only son.

Jon cleared his throat.

"Doctor Davies agrees with you, Vic. He's going to refer Emily to a specialist for tests." His eyebrows furrowed, and a pained expression filled his eyes.

"Oh my God. Oh my God," I cried, grabbing Jon's arm to steady myself.

I'd been saying she was sick for weeks, and Jon insisted I was overprotective, but I knew. Call it mother's intuition— call it what the hell you like— but I knew.

"Hey, come here, Vic. It still might be nothing." Jonathan pulled me into his arms.

I buried my head into his chest, trying to seek comfort from the familiar scent of him. But I could hear his heart hammering, and I knew he too was terrified.

"I'm confused," Frank said. "What does this mean?"

"Let's not speculate, Dad. Best to wait for the specialist's verdict."

***

After putting Emily to bed, I ran a bath. Then I lay immersed in coconut-scented bubbles until I was shivering cold and my skin was in danger of becoming as wrinkled as a walnut.

Wrapped in a fleecy dressing gown with my long brown hair twisted in a towel, I popped my head into Emily's room. She was asleep. I crept to her side and bent to kiss the top of her head and my stomach contracted.

As I turned to leave, a little voice whispered, "Goodnight, Mummy."

"Goodnight, my precious girl. I love you."

"How much?"

"To the moon and back."

Emily's tinkling laughter filled my ears and broke my heart.

I closed the door behind me, and then turned, pressing my back against it and sighing noisily.

A movement down the hallway made me turn with a start.

Frank stood half-in, half-out of his bedroom door, eyeing me, tentatively.

Frank was over six feet tall with broad shoulders, a rugged complexion and a head of thick greying hair. He was still a handsome and distinguished looking man despite the ravages of the stroke. Always very capable and powerful, he'd run the farm single-handed for years, only employing casual staff at the busiest times.

He'd also had a homekill butchery business that he'd operated from a converted old stone barn at the back of the property.

Finding himself bed-bound and helpless had almost been enough to kill him in itself, but between us, we'd managed. Now he was slowly regaining some independence.

"Hi, Frank."

"Sorry to disturb you. I keep intruding on your private moments."

"Don't be silly. You're as much a part of this as anyone." I pulled the towel from my head and threw it over my shoulder, running my fingers through my wet hair.

"She'll be fine, lass. Jon's right. We should wait and see what they say at the hospital."

I nodded, my lips trembling. "I've got a bad feeling about this, Frank."

"Come here." He walked towards me, his walking stick supporting his weak right side. I met him halfway, drawing strength from his calm, controlled, all-encompassing hug.

Frank was the closest thing I had to a parent. Both of mine had died years ago, leaving me feeling alone and abandoned at an early age. I had no other family, none that I knew of anyway. Maybe there were some distant cousins knocking about in Puerto Rico, where I was born, but nobody significant.

Frank cleared his throat. "You okay now?"

"Yes, thanks. I needed that," I said.

"There are plenty more where that came from, you know."

I smiled at him. "Come on. I'll race you downstairs. Last one down makes a cuppa."

I sped off, listening to him rant and curse, and then chuckle.

End of Sample

An Impossible Dilemma is available in paperback or kindle download from Amazon.

Printed in Great Britain
by Amazon